# The Ridicul

# Sidebottom and McPlop

ADRIAN LOBLEY

Children's Books by Adrian Lobley

Humour
The Ridiculous Adventures of Sidebottom and McPlop

Historical Fiction
Kane and the Mystery of the Missing World Cup
Kane and the Christmas Football Adventure

Educational - Maths
The Football Maths Book
The Football Maths Book - The Rematch!
The Football Maths Book - The Christmas Match
The Football Maths Book - The Birthday Party
The Football Maths Book - The World Cup

Educational - Reading
A Learn to Read Book - The Football Match
A Learn to Read Book - The Tennis Match

For Sebastian

First published in 2018

ACKNOWLEDGMENTS

With thanks to Sebastian, Matthew, Dad, Mum, Sarah, Kaden, Callan, Asher, Logan and Derry for reviewing and providing feedback on the book and cover.

Cover and illustrations by Peter Hudspith

# The Beginning

"Dad, come quick, look at this out of the window!" My nine year old shouted from the kitchen. "A man has just pulled that pole and sign out of our next door neighbour's garden and is running away with it!"

I wandered over, not in the least bit surprised to hear that somebody had pulled one of the estate agent signs out of the ground.

"Does he have black hair, is really plump and waddles as he runs?" I asked as I came to stand next to my son.

"Ha. Yes. How did you know?"

"Because that'll be McPlop. He's one of the two estate agents who's trying to sell the Jones's house." I peered through the window and could now see McPlop heading toward the field at the end of the road carrying the pole and sign above his head.

"So why has he run off with his own sign?"

"He hasn't. That sign has 'Sidebottom - Estate Agency' written on it. Sidebottom is his big rival and is the other estate agent who's trying to sell the Jones's house. If McPlop gets rid of Sidebottom's sign and just leaves his own sign there, he has more chance of selling the house and earning money.

"He's running towards the hedge and looks like he's going to launch the sign like a javelin into the middle of that muddy field." My son observed. We watched as the wooden pole and sign were launched high through the air. It did a perfect arc and landed with a splat in the field.

McPlop, having watched the sign land, looked very satisfied with himself. He clapped the mud from his hands, straightened his jacket and wandered off, whistling, as though nothing had happened.

"Won't he get into trouble for doing that?"

"Only if Sidebottom gets to hear about it." I chuckled. "He may well find out about it as they both live on our street so if someone spotted it they're bound to tell Sidebottom." I looked back up the street to see who was around. "Ha! Look who it is!" I exclaimed as I saw a tall man wearing glasses coming down the road, "Sidebottom himself! He looks furious as well. Ha! He must have seen McPlop rip out his sign." I nudged my son. "Come on let's watch what happens."

Sidebottom stormed into our neighbour's garden. He then ran at top speed towards McPlop's estate agency sign and launched a karate kick at it. He soared through the air shouting, 'Heeee-ya!' and thumped his foot against the middle of the wooden pole. It cracked and the top half hung to one side.

"What's he doing now?" My son asked.

Sidebottom had taken out a big black marker pen from his pocket and was in the process of crossing out some of the current wording and writing something onto the sign.

"I can just make it out," I said as I

squinted to get a better look, "It used to say 'McPlop Estate Agency' but Sidebottom has rewritten it so that it now says 'McPlop - Dooffus Estate Agent'."

"He he," giggled my son.

"What a pair of clowns," I said, shaking my head.

"Do they do things like that often?"

"All the time. It's quite funny actually. They're always sabotaging each other's plans. You would find it hilarious, the stupid things they do. Some of the stories would make you laugh your socks off." I sipped my cup of tea.

"Can I hear some of the stories?" My son pleaded.

"Go on then." We both wandered into the living room and I sat down on the sofa. "Sit down here and I'll tell you all about the ridiculous adventures of Sidebottom and McPlop."

# Sidebottom goes flying

I was on my driveway one Sunday morning and had just finished washing my car when Sidebottom wandered over from his house towards me.

"Morning, Mr Langley!" he said cheerfully. "You will never guess what..."

"I'm all ears, Sidebottom." I replied as I squeezed the water out of the cloth that I had just washed the car with.

"Look at me, can you guess?"

I hung the cloth on a peg inside my garage to dry and then turned to look at Sidebottom who was now standing right next to me.

"Sidebottom, why are you wearing those big brown goggles?" I frowned as I looked at what he was dressed in. "And why are you wearing that leather flying jacket, brown boots and have a scarf slung round your neck? You look like a World War I fighter pilot...but without the ability to fly a plane."

"That's where you're wrong though, Mr Langley," said Sidebottom triumphantly, "I've been on a five day course to learn how to fly a plane."

I narrowed my eyes at him.

"Sidebottom, it takes ages to learn how to fly a plane. Which course was it you went on?"

"Well...it was more of a 'flight simulator' that I went on."

"A flight simulator? Wow. You mean you were sitting in a simulator that was exactly like the inside of an aeroplane cabin and there were loads of screens around you which displayed the airport and runway?"

"Well...there was just one screen really."

I studied Sidebottom for a few seconds.

"Sidebottom, was this screen by any chance attached to your Playstation?"

"Um, possibly, Mr Langley."

"And this 'simulator'....was it just a 'flight simulator' game on your Playstation."

"Um, again, yes."

"So basically you've just spent five days on the Playstation and now you think you can fly a real plane."

"That's right, Mr Langley!" Sidebottom seemed very pleased with himself.

I shook my head in despair.

"What are those books tucked under your arm?" I asked as I pointed at them. Sidebottom took the first book out from under his arm and read its cover.

"This one's called 'How to fly a plane'." He then read the cover of the second book. "This one's called 'Flying for Dummies'."

"Well, they got the last one right, at least." I replied. Sidebottom was completely oblivious to the comment.

"So far I've read the first three chapters Mr Langley, but I think flying a plane's going to be easy as apparently there's an 'autopilot', so instead of doing all the flying I can just get the plane's computer to do it."

"Aaargh, Sidebottom. The autopilot is

for when you're up in the air and just going in a straight line. What about taking off and landing? As the pilot, you have to put down the landing gear?"

"The landing gear? What's the landing gear?"

"The wheels, Sidebottom! The wheels!"

"Ah. 'Landing the plane' must be in Chapter Four of the book, Mr Langley. I'm only on Chapter Three."

I rolled my eyes.

"Why don't you come and see me fly, Mr Langley. I'm heading to the small airport up the road because an instructor's going to let me pilot his plane. I've reassured him that I'm an expert so he seemed happy on the phone for me to start flying straightaway."

"Oh my goodness, Sidebottom." I said, shaking my head. I then thought about it a little more. The idea of watching Sidebottom attempting to fly a plane would actually be quite a sight.

"Do you know what, Sidebottom? I would love to come to watch you in action."

"Excellent, Mr Langley, let's go straight away!"

A few minutes later we were in Sidebottom's old car, which was a complete hunk of junk, on the way to the local airport. Smoke billowed out of the back of the dilapidated old car as other cars beeped at us because of all the black fumes floating down the road. No one could see a thing.

After an embarrasing five minute journey we turned the corner into the small aeroclub and headed for the parking spaces. There was an engineer working on one of the planes as we drove in. As Sidebottom pulled the car to a stop near him not far from the airfield, the exhaust produced its now usual BANG. The poor engineer, who had his head under the bonnet of the plane because he was working on an intricate part of the engine, almost leapt out of his skin. He whacked his head against the underside of the bonnet and all his spanners clattered to the ground. Sidebottom was completely oblivious. He sprung out of the car and wandered past the engineer.

"Morning," he said cheerily to the poor mechanic who was rubbing the back of his head.

"Sorry about that," I muttered to the man as I passed him.

I looked around the aeroclub. It was made up of an open hangar that contained another three planes, there was also a small building next to it and then a single runway stretching from one end of the airfield to the other.

"I'm going to get a coffee from the aeroclub," I said as I caught up with Sidebottom, "I can watch you from there."

"Excellent." Sidebottom replied as he strode over the grass in the direction of a man who I assumed was the flying instructor.

As I entered the building I ordered a coffee and then positioned myself on the seats facing out to the runway. After a couple of minutes I could hear the sound of a propeller firing up but looking out through the window, I couldn't see the plane yet. Then all of a sudden it appeared. It was purple and came zooming out from behind the hangar but instead of going in a straight line along the runway it seemed to be zig-zagging all over the place.

"What on earth is going on with that plane?" said the man sitting next to me in the aeroclub building. He was peering out of the window in wonder at what the instructor's plane was doing.

"That will be Sidebottom." I said, fairly unsurprised.

At that point, the plane wheels lifted up off the ground and then after a few seconds bounced back down again. Then the plane went up again, before slamming down into the concrete runway and bouncing back up into the air once more. The plane was now flying really close to the building that I was having my coffee in. So close in fact that I could see the instructor's face inside the plane. He was completely white - like he was going to have a heart attack. Meanwhile I could see Sidebottom who was beaming with delight, no doubt thrilled at how he well he thought he was piloting the plane.

"Who's Sidebottom?" The man next to me said, before remembering something the instructor had mentioned to him earlier. "Oh wait, he told me he was taking a guy flying today who had said to him that he was a bit of an 'expert pilot'."

"Ha. Yes, that will be Sidebottom." I laughed.

"He doesn't look like much of an an expert to me," said the man. The plane rebounded off the tarmac again with the instructor clinging on for dear life. "Where did this 'Sidebottom' guy do his training?"

"On his Playstation." I replied.

"They're going to crash aren't they?" the man said, his eyes glued to the plane.

"No such luck. I suspect Sidebottom will survive completely intact, without a scratch on him." I replied.

Just then, the plane took off! It swooped upwards from the runway at an incredibly steep angle. We could see the instructor's face appear at the window. He seemed to be shouting for help as the plane soared almost vertically into the sky.

"I think the instructor might pack in giving flying lessons after this. I've never seen him look so scared," said the man next to me.

"Ha. This is nothing. That was the easy bit. You wait until Sidebottom tries to land."

"You think he'll be able to do it?"

"Only, if he remembers to put the wheels down," I replied, "believe me, there's no guarantee he'll remember."

As we talked we watched the plane bank to the left and circle around, ready to come in to try and land. The instructor by now was slumped deep into the passenger seat. We could only see the top of his head. When his face did pop up, he looked like he was having a nervous breakdown.

"Here he comes!" I said grinning as I watched Sidebottom. "Get ready for this corker."

The plane seemed to be descending at a steady rate and then all of a sudden it dived downwards so the plane was heading almost vertically towards the ground.

"A tenner says Sidebottom has just turned off the autopilot." I chuckled as I sipped my coffee. "I wish I'd brought some popcorn with me. This is great viewing."

At the last second, the instructor sprung into action, grabbed the controls from Sidebottom, pulled the stick back and the plane pulled up just in time. It roared along the runway and the pilot touched the plane down with a jolt. After a few minutes the plane taxied to a stop by the hanger.

Sidebottom leapt down from the plane whooping and hollering and doing a little dance.

"Woo hoo!" he shouted. "That was

brilliant, Mr Langley!" he shouted in my direction. Meanwhile the instructor climbed unsteadily down from the plane and bent down to kiss the ground. He then curled up in a ball, tucking his legs up into his body. He rocked backwards and forwards on the ground and started sobbing.

"I see Sidebottom has surpassed himself again." I said to the man next to me.

The following day I was tending to the flowers in my front garden and chuckling to myself at Sidebottom's antics at the aeroclub the day before. It was around this time that McPlop wandered up to me, on his way from his house.

"Morning, Mr Langley."

"Ah, McPlop, how are we today?" I finished tipping the contents of my watering can onto the last of the flowers.

"Very well, Mr Langley. I'm walking into town for a spot of shopping. Would you be interested in joining me?"

I leant on my pitchfork, which had its

three prongs spiked into the ground, as I considered McPlop's offer.

"Well, yes I do need a few things. Okay, give me a couple of minutes and I'll join you."

After swapping my gardening shoes for some trainers I joined McPlop and we headed out of the cul-de-sac and towards the shops. As we walked, McPlop told me of all the new customers he had recently got and he pointed down the road where I could see lots of houses all with 'McPlop Estate Agency' signs outside them.

"Very impressive, McPlop," I commented as we began walking past them, "there must be fifteen of your signs in a row here." McPlop beamed with pride as I complimented him.

As we walked on I relayed the story of Sidebottom attempting to fly a plane the previous day, much to McPlop's horror.

"He's lucky to be alive,"

"Indeed." I replied. "Not only that but after just ten minutes flying in a plane with Sidebottom, the flying instructor has given up flying for life."

"So what's the instructor doing now?"

"Apparently he just sits in a chair in a dark room rocking backwards and forwards saying the words 'Pull up Sidebottom! Pull up Sidebottom! Pull up Sidebottom!' over and over." McPlop tutted at the story as I continued, "I don't think he's very well."

We had wandered past the last of McPlop's fifteen signs but all of a sudden McPlop started sniffing the air around him. "What's that smell, Mr Langley?"

"Cowpats in the field, McPlop,"I said, as I looked at all the cows at the other side of the hedge next to us. One of the cows was doing a poo as we looked over. The poo slopped onto the ground into a swirly pile. There was quite a smell. "Loads of cowpats, look at them all."

"Wow." McPlop said, surveying the field.

Just then, we could hear the sound of an engine. I looked in the sky. It was something ahead in the distance. I could just make it out.

"A plane," I commented in the general direction, "it seems to be flying this way." As it got a little nearer I noticed the colour. It was purple. "I recognise that plane. That's the instructor's plane from yesterday."

"I thought he'd given up flying though?" said McPlop.

"That was my understanding." The plane, which was heading towards us, was now getting closer and seemed to be stuttering, as though it was running out of fuel or the pilot wasn't a very good pilot. It suddenly nosedived as it headed straight towards the road that McPlop and I were walking on.

"Oh my goodness, it looks like he's going to try and land on this road!" I gasped.

The plane was plummeting to the ground just like it had the day before. Just as it was about to crash the pilot must have pulled the stick back as the plane pulled sharply up.

"It's flying only a few feet above the road and heading straight for us! Save yourself McPlop!" I shouted as I ran over to the hedge at the side I was walking on.

McPlop took my instructions very seriously but instead of just moving to the side of the road and standing next to me so he was safe from the plane, he ran straight past me, took a running jump and dived over the hedge.

"Noooo, McPlop!" I shouted as he soared through the air in front of me. "The cowpats are in that field!"

SPLAT!

McPlop landed head first into three of the biggest freshest smelliest cow pats in the whole field. He slid through the cowpats as he landed and skidded towards the swirly cowpat that we had just seen being laid. "Nooo!" McPlop shouted as his face rocketed towards it, unable to stop.

SPLAT!

McPlop's face landed right in the swirly monster cowpat.

McPlop stood up and wiped the poo from his eyes.

He looked to the road and saw the plane, which was now roaring past us both at head height. He looked at the pilot.

"Sidebottom?" muttered McPlop. He then looked further along the road at his fifteen precious estate agency signs. The plane was heading towards them.

Sidebottom was locked onto his targets, namely McPlop's signs. The wing of the plane hit the first sign and disintegrated it. A millisecond later it hit the next sign and that was sliced right in half, then the third, then the fourth. Within a couple of seconds the plane had chopped all fifteen of McPlop's signs in half.

"Result!!" yelled Sidebottom out of the pilot's window and thumped his fist into the air in joy.

"Sidebottom!!" Yelled McPlop. Sidebottom couldn't hear him though as he was now long gone.

A car was approaching the plane head

on now, so Sidebottom pulled the plane up sharply into the air and away from the road, with Sidebottom laughing hysterically as he headed back to the airfield.

McPlop started blubbering as he wiped the poo from his face and trudged through the cowpats to return home.

# The Sidebottom and McPlop Estate Agency

It was a summer Sunday and I was asleep in bed when I was woken by the sunlight streaming through a gap in the curtains. It felt like a good morning for a bacon sandwich so I dressed quickly and went downstairs. The lounge curtains were closed so the first thing I did was wander over and pull them apart.

I jumped back in shock. There was someone standing outside my lounge window looking in!

"Sidebottom!" I exclaimed, as I realised who it was. "What on earth are you doing standing at my window?" I mouthed at him through the window pane. Sidebottom had a big beaming smile. He seemed particularly pleased with himself. I leaned forward and opened the big window.

"Well, Sidebottom, what is it?" I said

impatiently

"Great news, Mr Langley. I have a plan!"

"Brilliant," I said rolling my eyes, "you've just scared the living daylights out of me to tell me you have a plan?" Sidebottom stood there grinning.

"I know I'm going to regret asking this," I sighed, "go on, what is it? What's your big plan?"

"Well," he said, "I've decided to ask McPlop if he wants to begin a joint estate agency with me." Sidebottom nodded at his idea as he thought about how great the idea was. "Think about it Mr Langley! It will be called 'The Sidebottom and McPlop Estate Agency'." Sidebottom explained as he imagined the name lit up in bright lights in front of him. "In fact, I'm going to go and wake McPlop up now and tell him my brilliant idea."

"Good!" I said. "Yes, why don't you go and stand outside his lounge window. You could scare the daylights out of him too."

Sidebottom seemed to love the idea of scaring McPlop so he set off over to McPlop's house and stood outside his front window. "Unbelievable" I muttered to myself as I headed for the kitchen to make myself a bacon sandwich.

I had a pleasant couple of hours of peace and quiet. Then there was a knock at the door.

"Not Sidebottom again." I groaned as I trudged over to the door and opened it. Standing there were Sidebottom and McPlop.

"Fantastic news, Mr Langley," said Sidebottom gleefully. "McPlop has agreed to join me to make 'The Sidebottom and McPlop Estate Agency'." I just shrugged at this piece of irrelevant news.

"Wait a minute," said McPlop. "Why is it your name first, Sidebottom? It should be my name first. It should be 'The McPlop and Sidebottom Estate Agency'."

"No it jolly well should not!" said Sidebottom indignantly. "I invented the idea therefore it should be my name first.

It should be 'The Sidebottom and McPlop Estate Agency'."

"McPlop should be first!" shouted McPlop, with no real justification for why his name should be first.

"Only an idiot would put McPlop first!" shouted Sidebottom

"Garbage! 'McPlop' is the greatest!" shouted McPlop.

"Sidebottom first, imbecile!" yelled back Sidebottom at the top of his voice, despite McPlop only standing a few inches from him.

"Stop! Stop!" I shouted at them both. The pair halted and stared at me as I continued to speak. "Fascinating conversation though this is, I have to go out." I picked up my car keys from the table by my door, closed the front door behind me and headed for my car. "I will leave you both to your highly intellectual debate." The pair turned and looked at one another.

"McPlop first!" shouted McPlop.

"Sidebottom!" shouted Sidebottom. I

shook my head in despair.

Then all of a sudden, to my shock, McPlop and Sidebottom started wrestling!

"McPlop!" shouted McPlop as he grabbed hold of Sidebottom and dragged him down onto my muddy lawn using a wrestling move he had seen on television.

"Sidebottom!" shouted Sidebottom, as he crashed down to the ground splatting in the mud with McPlop on top of him.

"Pffft-McPlop" shouted McPlop as he got some mud in his mouth. He rolled Sidebottom towards the muddiest bit of the lawn.

"Sidebott..." Sidebottom's face landed smack in the mud puddle before he could finish what he was saying.

"McPl..." Shouted McPlop at the exact moment that Sidebottom picked up some mud and tried to stuff it in McPlop's mouth.

I watched in total surprise as the two grown men rolled back and forth trying to find the muddiest bit of the lawn to shove the other one's face into.

Then McPlop got to his feet, shortly followed by Sidebottom. The pair looked at each other.

"It should be 'The Sidebottom and McPlop Estate Agency'," said Sidebottom, brushing some of the mud off and straightening his shirt.

"That's the most ridiculous name I've ever heard of!" countered McPlop. " 'The McPlop and Sidebottom Estate Agency' is miles better! In fact it's one of the greatest names ever invented."

"You buffoon, McPlop," said Sidebottom. "Any more of this imbecility and we ditch the name 'McPlop' out of the title completely!" Threatened Sidebottom. "Anyway, McPlop sounds like someone going to the toilet."

McPlop ran at Sidebottom and launched a full rugby tackle on him "McPllllllopppp first!" McPlop shouted as the pair went crashing back into the mud.

"Never!" shouted Sidebottom

"I give up!" I shouted at the pair of them. They had wrecked my front garden.

"I'm going to the shop." Neither of the men heard though as they were now attempting some kind of Sumo wrestling moves where they were trying to grab the other person's underpants and yank them up out of their trousers.

"Wedgie!" shouted Sidebottom as he pulled McPlops pants upwards.

"Ooooooo!" squeaked McPlop, feeling the full force of the wedgie.

I reversed the car out of my drive and set off down the road. Ahead of me by the edge of the pavement I could see two estate agents signs. The first one was McPlop's and the second one was Sidebottom's. I smiled.

"Right, this will teach you to destroy my front garden." I muttered to myself. I mounted the pavement with the car and smashed firstly into McPlop's sign and then Sidebottom's. The wooden signs went flying up into the air.

"Take that buffoons!!" I shouted with great glee as I drove off into the sunset laughing hysterically.

# Sidebottom the fireman

It was three o'clock in the afternoon one Saturday when there was a knock at my door.

"I really hope this isn't either of those dunces, McPlop or Sidebottom," I thought to myself, "I was just about to sit down and watch some television." I walked across my front room and peered through the little hole in the front door to see who it was.

"Interesting, a fireman." I mumbled to myself. So I opened the door. Lo and behold, who should it be, dressed in a firemans uniform...

"Sidebottom," I sighed. I shook my head in dismay at having opened the door. I had a sinking feeling already. "Go on then, enlighten me as to why you're dressed as a fireman."

"Because I AM a fireman, Mr Langley! I've just signed up!" Sidebottom yelped.

He was clearly very pleased with himself.

"Sidebottom, believe me, if I was trapped in a burning building, the last person I would want to see hurtling towards me in a huge fire engine....is you." Sidebottom still had a huge grin on his face.

"But what if it was your hedge that was on fire, Mr Langley, or one of McPlop's estate agency signs was on fire. I could easily put those out with the hose on the fire engine."

"Sidebottom, if there is one thing that you would not do, it would be to rescue one of McPlop's estate agency signs if it was on fire." I let out another sigh. "In fact, I would be surprised if it hadn't been you who would have set McPlop's sign alight in the first place." I looked at Sidebottom, who was now grinning a big white toothy smile. I then thought about what he had just said, "Hang on a minute, Sidebottom, why would my hedge be on fire?"

"I'm just saying....IF it was on fire."

"Yes Sidebottom, and I'm saying 'WHY would it be on fire?'"

"It could spontaneously combust?" Sidebottom suggested, seeming pleased with his explanation.

"So you mean that my hedge might suddenly set itself on fire for no reason whatsoever?"

"It happens in Australia, Mr Langley." He clicked his fingers as he remembered, "I've seen it on television."

"Aargh, Sidebottom, that's because the temperature in Australia would have been scorchingly hot and someone started the fire. We're in Britain - it's cold and raining most of the time." I blew out my cheeks. My Saturday afternoon was whizzing by here. "Now listen here, Sidebottom, I'm going to go back to watching my television program. I don't want to hear any more stupid stories about fires and firemen. Okay?"

"Ah, okay, Mr Langley." He looked a bit confused. "So what should I do now, Mr Langley?"

"Well I suggest you go back to the fire station, explain to them that you're a confused Estate Agent who's having a mid-life crisis and thinks he's a fireman, and then hand them back their fireman's outfit."

"Ah, yes Mr Langley sir. A good idea, I'll do that."

"Good. Goodbye Sidebottom." I shut the door and settled back into my chair and switched the television on.

After about thirty minutes though I saw some orange flickering outside my window and my hallway started filling with smoke. I ran to the front door and flung it open. There before my eyes was my hedge which was on fire!

"SIDEBOTTOM!!!!!" I yelled at the top of my voice.

From behind a tree at the other side of the road Sidebottom peeked out. I could only see his head, which he tilted to the side when he heard me.

"Everything okay, Mr Langley?" enquired Sidebottom very calmly as though he hadn't noticed my hedge on fire.

"No it isn't okay!! My hedge is on fire, you idiot!" I watched as the huge orange flames licked higher and higher and the fire spread. "Do something, you buffoon, you're supposed to be a fireman!"

"I handed my fireman's uniform back though, Mr Langley." He scratched his chin. "I do have an idea of how to put it out though."

"What's the idea?" I screamed. "Quick! I won't have a hedge left at this rate." As soon as I had stopped yelling at him, he ran into a neighbour's garden that had one of McPlop's estate agency signs in it and yanked the sign out of the ground. Sidebottom then ran over to my hedge and started bashing the hedge with the sign."

"Sidebottom," I said quietly in disbelief, "what on earth are you doing?" My mouth was wide open.

"I thought that if I bash the hedge with one of McPlop's sign's it might put the fire out."

"Sidebottom." I said.

"Yes, Mr Langley."

"You're an idiot."

"Yes, Mr Langley."

"And another thing Sidebottom....you started this fire, didn't you?"

"Um, I might have done, Mr Langley."

I groaned.

Sidebottom kept on bashing the hedge with McPlop's sign which was now half hanging off the wooden stake and was pretty much destroyed. "I'm sure it's working, Mr Langley. Look if I bash the bit of the hedge that isn't yet on fire, the fire might not spread to it."

"Sidebottom," I said calmly, "have you got another sign?"

"Ah! Do you want to help, Mr Langley. Of course. I'll get one." Sidebottom sprinted to another neighbour's garden, ripped out another of McPlop's signs and ran back with it.

"Pass it here." I said. Sidebottom handed it over.

"Right, it's clobbering time Sidebottom!" I shouted and ran after him waving McPlop's estate agency sign furiously in his direction. Sidebottom saw me coming. He immediately ditched McPlop's sign by throwing it into the fire and then ran for the hills.

"Sorry Mr Langley!!" he cried as he ran away as fast as he could.

"Imbecile!" I shouted as I chased after him waving McPlop's sign in his direction.

# Roadtrip

It was a balmy summer day and I had just finished mowing my front lawn and putting the lawn mower back into the shed, when I heard a call from behind me.

"Hello, Mr Langley!"

"Ah, Sidebottom" I said as I turned around to see who it was. "McPlop as well. Aren't I lucky?" I said as I rolled my eyes.

"Very lucky," replied Sidebottom, who nodded at McPlop. "We have had a brilliant idea, Mr Langley!"

"Another one, Sidebottom?"

"Yes, Mr Langley, so that is now two brilliant ideas this week," he said proudly.

"Go on then, Sidebottom, what is it this time?" I said, with an impending feeling of doom.

"You, me and McPlop could all go for a roadtrip!" McPlop nodded enthusiastically as Sidebottom spoke.

"A roadtrip?"

"I've got a new car, Mr Langley? We could take it out for a drive to the seaside, with the music on, the windows down and the wind in our hair."

I paused and thought about it for a minute.

"Alright, I could do with a break. Let me get my jacket and we'll head out for a drive. Where's your car, Sidebottom?" I asked.

"Just around the corner, Mr Langley." So the three of us walked out of my driveway, along the pavement and round the bend.

"There's nothing here Sidebottom, except for some rusty old banger that needs to towed off to the junkyard."

"That's the car I've just bought, Mr Langley!" Said Sidebottom proudly as walked over to it and patted his hand on the front wing of the car. The front wing, which was covered in rust and looked about fifty years old, promptly snapped off as Sidebottom touched it, and went clattering to the ground making a huge noise. "It's a great runner!" said Sidebottom, seemingly unfazed by the state of his new purchase.

"Let's give it a try, Sidebottom!" said McPlop.

"I must be mad," I groaned as I followed McPlop over to Sidebottom's new vehicle.

"I've made some great modifications, Mr Langley," Sidebottom explained as the three of us tried to squeeze into the little Mini. I've had a bigger engine fitted."

"I must be insane." I muttered to myself as I climbed into the front passenger seat and McPlop crammed into the back.

"I've also fitted a brilliant new stereo system and big loud speakers," Sidebottom said with a grin.

"I should be sent to the loony bin." I mumbled.

"Right, let's go!" said Sidebottom and put his key in the ignition.

"Just one question," McPlop said, "does this car have a toilet?"

"McPlop, this car IS a toilet." I pointed out.

"No, it doesn't have a toilet," Sidebottom replied, ignoring my comment, "but that's a brilliant idea, McPlop, I will make sure I get one fitted the instant we return."

I pulled a face of utter disbelief and was about to question how on earth Sidebottom would fit a toilet into a mini.

"I'm not even going to ask," I said, shaking my head in general resignation at the whole conversation.

"We're off!" shouted Sidebottom, and

with that he thumped his foot down on the accelerator. The little car shot down the road at a surprisingly quick pace.

"Slow down, Sidebottom!" I yelled as we flew around the first corner with the little car almost tipping over. The tyres were screeching against the road surface as they clung desperately onto their wheel rims. Sidebottom hit the straight road, slammed the gear stick forward into third gear and pushed his foot harder onto the accelerator.

"Sidebottom!!" I shouted as I gripped my hands onto my seat belt.

"Ah my stereo, Mr Langley, I nearly forgot." With that, Sidebottom ramped up the volume on his sound system until music pumped out of his new powerful car speakers. The music was now blasting out and Sidebottom opened all the windows in the car.

The stereo boomed out its bass, "Boom! Boom!, Boom!" I couldn't hear a thing. The poor neighbours we streaked past wondered what on earth was going on. Three men in a little mini that sounded like it was going to explode.

"Aarrghh, Sidebottom!!" I shouted. "Slow down!"

"What?" shouted Sidebottom as he pumped his head up and down to the sound of his music.

"Slow dowwwwnnnn, Sidebottom!!" I shouted even louder.

"I can't hear you, Mr Langley, because of the music!" shouted Sidebottom as loudly as he could and pointing at the radio.

"Turn it down then, Sidebottom, you idiot!" I yelled back. I then gripped the handle by my seat as Sidebottom tore around the next corner almost destroying one of McPlop's estate agent signs that was outside a house.

"Blast. I missed it," muttered Sidebottom to himself. "I'll get the next one," he thought and gave McPlop a grin. McPlop grinned back, although he wasn't quite sure why Sidebottom was grinning at him. "There you go, Mr Langley."

Sidebottom said as he turned the volume down from 'Ridiculously Loud' to just 'Loud', "what was it you were saying?"

At that moment Sidebottom tried to overtake a long bus by veering around it into the path of the traffic that was coming in the opposite direction.

"Aagghh, Sidebottom, we're on the wrong side of the road!!" I shouted, as I saw a car hurtling towards us. Sidebottom veered back in behind the bus in the nick of time.

"Sorry, Mr Langley. I just thought I would find out whether the road was clear."

"You idiot, Sidebottom, you're supposed to look first, not just drive straight into the traffic!"

"Good point Mr Langley, I'll try that next time."

I shook my head in despair.

The bus then turned left, out of our way, so Sidebottom thumped his foot on the accelerator again. The little car roared with its new engine and Sidebottom launched it round the next corner. All of a sudden the other front wing started rattling. It was coming loose.

"The front wing Sidebottom!" I shouted as the front part of the car flew off, soared up into the air and went skidding off down the road in the opposite direction.

"It's okay, Mr Langley, we've lost both front wings now so the car looks even," said Sidebottom, trying to reassure me.

"The bonnet, Sidebottom!" shouted McPlop from the back seat as he saw the bonnet clasp unfasten and the bonnet come completely up and land over the front windscreen.

"I can't see anything!" said Sidebottom, who was now beginning to panic a little. He stuck his head out of the open window so he could see where he was going.

"Hit the brakes, Sidebottom!" I yelled, almost sure we were all going to die.

"I'm going to be sick," moaned McPlop who was in the seat directly behind me.

"Not over me you're, not McPlop!" I

shouted at him. I pointed at Sidebottom. "If you have to be sick over anyone, do it over Sidebottom."

"I'll try, Mr Langley." McPlop replied, looking almost green now.

"I'm going to hit the brakes, Mr Langley."

"Never mind telling me you're going to hit the brakes, just hit them Sidebottom!!"

With that, Sidebottom slammed his foot on the brakes but nothing happened.

"The foot brake doesn't work, Mr Langley!" We were still flying down the road with Sidebottom sticking his head out of the window to see where he was going.

Such was his concern with the situation, Sidebottom let out a huge noisy trump.

"Uuurgh, Sidebottom," shouted McPlop, who felt the full force of the gas leak.

"Sidebottom," I said calmly, "when you said to McPlop that he would be going on a journey where he would have wind rushing through his hair, I don't think he envisaged that it would be your wind rushing through his hair." I shook my head. "Now why don't you try the hand brake, before we all get killed."

"Good idea." Sidebottom yanked the hand brake and the car came skidding to a halt.

"Bluuurrreeuuggghhh," said McPlop as he was sick all over Sidebottom.

I calmly opened my door.

"That's me done chaps. Thanks for the ride. I think I will walk back home if it's all the same with you. Cheerio!"

# Ice Cream Van Wars

It was a breezy Sunday and I was carrying a bag of compost from my back garden round to the front of my house. As I walked along the side of the house I was greeted by a most unusual sight. Blocking my driveway were two ice cream vans. Neither had their engines on and there were no drivers. I turned around the corner to the front of my house.

"Morning, Mr Langley!" Two voices shouted in unison, making me jump. I almost dropped my bag of compost.

"McPlop, Sidebottom." I groaned. "What do you two clowns want?" I looked at their clothes which consisted of matching white gowns with white hats.

"We're trying our luck at being ice cream van men!" said McPlop. I frowned as McPlop continued to speak. "We just thought we would come to tell you."

"Brilliant." I said sarcastically. "Can I suggest you both get into your ice cream vans and move them from the end of my driveway and go and sell some ice creams then!"

"Good idea, Mr Langley." said McPlop. "It's highly likely I will sell more ice creams than Sidebottom," stated McPlop very matter-of-factly.

"Pah!" responded Sidebottom. "In that old wreck of an ice cream van of yours," replied Sidebottom.

"It's better than than hunk of junk you drive around in and at least I have a van that plays a loud tune," McPlop pointed out.

"Enough! Enough!" I said. "Both of you, stop bickering." I held my hands up. "Now, who is going where? You can't both sell ice creams to the same streets. You need to decide who sells ice creams to the south of the village and who sells ice creams to the north of the village."

"Baggsy, the north!" shouted Sidebottom.

"Okay, I'll have the south then," said McPlop in a resigned tone.

I pointed at the vans. "Go!"

"We're off!" shouted McPlop. He promptly turned and sprinted up the driveway as fast as he could. "Too slow!" he shouted over his shoulder at Sidebottom.

Sidebottom shot after him. As he leapt into his driver's seat, McPlop was already gunning his van out of the cul de sac at high speed.

About twenty minutes later Sidebottom was parked in the middle of a housing estate. Unfortunately though he had purchased an ice cream van which didn't play a tune. This meant that none of the children in the houses knew that he was there. The horn didn't work either.

"No wonder, the man sold me this ice cream van so cheaply. If the tune doesn't play, I'm not going to be able to sell any ice cream," grumbled Sidebottom.

Meanwhile at the south side of the village McPlop was blaring his tune out of the big megaphone on the top of his ice cream van. He was doing a roaring trade. All the children were running out of the houses and over the grass verges towards his van.

Sidebottom could hear McPlop's ice cream tune blaring out from a mile away.

Sidebottom was fuming.

He would end up losing to McPlop.

"This is not good," he muttered to himself, "time to sort this out."

He rammed the gearstick forward, slammed his foot down on the accelerator and the ice cream van shot forwards and round the bend. Sidebottom floored it all the way to the south of the village and within minutes he came screeching round the corner of the estate that McPlop was parked in.

"Wow, look at all those customers!" Sidebottom exclaimed as he saw a huge queue of children in line at the side of McPlop's ice cream van. "There must be twenty kids wanting McPlop's ice creams." Sidebottom frowned. "Right, we'll see about this!"

He drove to within ten metres of McPlop's van and pulled on the handbrake. Sidebottom then stepped into the back section of his ice cream van, flipped the switch to start the ice cream machine and slid the side window back. He knew McPlop was charging three pounds for each of his ice creams.

"Get your ice creams for two pounds!" he shouted out of his van window. "One pound less than McPlop's!"

As soon as the kids heard Sidebottom's prices, every single child in the line sprinted as fast as they could from McPlop's queue, to form a new queue at Sidebottom's van.

"Brilliant!" shouted Sidebottom with a huge beaming smile on his face, as the last of the children appeared in a new line in front of him. He served the first child in line, "Would you like chocolate sauce on that, young man?" He asked him.

McPlop, who was serving a customer at the time, watched in amazement as all his other customers disappeared before his eyes. After he had finished serving his only customer, McPlop peered out of the window of his van and looked round to see all his customers at Sidebottom's van. He was furious.

"Right, two can play at that game!" McPlop cupped his hands around his mouth. "Ice creams for a pound!" He yelled at the top of his voice. "That's right, ice creams for just one pound. That's one pound cheaper than Sidebottom's. Plus they're better ice creams. Sidebottom's ice creams are rubbish."

As soon as McPlop had finished shouting, all the children in Sidebottom's queue sprinted back to McPlop's van and formed a new queue eagerly anticipating getting their ice creams for one pound each.

"Heh, heh," chuckled McPlop, "that will show Sidebottom. He won't offer an ice cream for less than a pound, unless he's a complete imbecile."

Just as McPlop had started serving the

first child in his newly restored queue, he heard a shout.

"Ice creams for free!" shouted Sidebottom from inside his van.

"Yaaay!" shouted the children as they charged back over to Sidebottom's.

"I don't believe it," McPlop said, his jaw dropping open, "that wazzock has stolen all my business again!"

Just then, McPlop had an idea.

He cupped his hands in front of his mouth one more time.

"I will pay every child, 'two pounds' if they buy an ice cream from me!"

"Woo hoo!" shouted the kids, "free cash!" They stormed back to form a queue at McPlop's.

Sidebottom couldn't bare it. McPlop had got all his customers back and was going to win the battle of the ice cream wars. He had to do something.

"No way are you going to beat me." Sidebottom muttered under his breath as he watched the kids disappear. Sidebottom leaned out of his window and shouted as loudly as he could, "I will pay you each four pounds for every ice cream you buy from me!"

McPlop grinned. He had wound Sidebottom up until his rival had lost the plot.

"Four pounds!" screamed the children with great joy as they sprinted from McPlop's van to Sidebottom's.

McPlop grinned to himself, closed the window on his van and went to sit in his driver's seat. He watched as every one of the twenty children in the queue walked off carrying as many of Sidebottom's ice creams as they could. After about twenty minutes McPlop had watched Sidebottom serving about four ice cream's to each of the twenty children.

"By my calculations," McPlop said to himself, "that imbecile Sidebottom has served eighty ice creams and will have had to pay each child four pounds for every ice cream." McPlop started chuckling to himself. "That's over three hundred pounds he's had to pay out!" McPlop howled with laughter.

In the other ice cream van, Sidebottom was getting more and more angry with every ice cream he was selling. He couldn't understand why every child was buying as many ice creams as they could but he knew it was costing him a lot of money.

"This is very odd," he thought, "I was sure I would make money selling ice creams."

After the last child had gone and Sidebottom had handed over all his spare money, he was red-faced with fury. He had just worked out what McPlop had done to him. He looked through the front window of his ice cream van to see McPlop doubled over with laughter and shouting, "Sidebottom, you turnip!"

At this point, to laud it over Sidebottom even more, McPlop climbed out of his van and wandered across to Sidebottom's vehicle.

Sidebottom was still livid but had worked out how to get his own back. As

McPlop came to the window of Sidebottom's van, Sidebottom slid back the window. He then adjusted the nozzle on the ice cream machine to face forward and turned the machine up to 'Maximum'. As McPlop walked up and stood in front of the window laughing, Sidebottom yanked the handle of the ice cream machine down hard. Ice cream jetted forwards out of the window, straight into McPlop's face.

SPLAT!

McPlop just stood there in shock as the ice cream carried on pelting him in the face. Sidebottom then grabbed the raspberry sauce bottle in one hand and the chocolate sauce in the other hand and squeezed the bottles as hard as he could at McPlop.

SPLAT!

McPlop was drenched in ice cream and sauce. The ice cream and sauce hit the ground, McPlop tried to move back, slipped on it and went sprawling onto the floor as the ice cream continued to churn out all over him from the machine.

After a few more seconds Sidebottom turned the machine off and then threw a thin wafer down on top of McPlop which landed on his head to make him look like a human strawberry and chocolate ice cream sundae.

"Ha, ha, ha!" Laughed Sidebottom as he returned to his driver's seat and gunned his ice cream van out of the estate.

# Sidebottom and McPlop go to the Supermarket

It was a fine sunny morning when there was a knock on my front door. I was expecting a parcel to arrive so opened the door feeling quite excited at the visit of the postman. My face soon dropped. It wasn't the post man.

"Sidebottom." I groaned

"Mr Langley!" Sidebottom said. "How would you like to go out for a trip?"

"I wouldn't, Sidebottom."

"But we could go to the supermarket!" Sidebottom seemed very excited about this revolutionary idea.

"That's not really going for a trip, Sidebottom. More of a food-shop." I considered it for a moment. "However, I do actually need some food. Alright, go on then." I grabbed my jacket and checked my keys and wallet were inside the pocket. "Come on. We might as well go in my car."

"Yippee!" Squealed Sidebottom.

After a ten minute drive we arrived at the supermarket and as I parked the car, Sidebottom jumped out and ran across the car park like an excited child. He shouted back to me as he charged at full pelt, "I'm going to try on the fancy dress costumes, Mr Langley! They sell super hero costumes at this supermarket!"

I shook my head as I watched him disappear into the supermarket. I then locked the car and trailed after him.

As I walked in the entrance I could see some people gathering at the bottom of the two escalators. There was a bit of a commotion, so I made my way over to see what was happening. As I pushed through the crowd of people in front of me I could see a man running up the 'down escalator'. He was running as fast as he could up the escalator but as the escalator was going just as fast downwards he wasn't actually getting anywhere.

"Sidebottom, you idiot!" I shouted.

"Ah! Mr Langley" Sidebottom panted, clearly out of breath from all the running, "I can't get up this escalator!"

"Sidebottom, that's the wrong escalator! To get to the upper floor you need to go on the 'Up escalator'!" I put my head in my hands.

"What?" shouted Sidebottom as he looked over at the 'Up escalator' that was right next to the one he was on, "so I should be on that one?" he said pointing at the other escalator as he continued running.

"Yes you buffoon. You need to be on the other one, where all the other people are." I yelled back.

All of a sudden, Sidebottom leapt sideways over the black handrails between the escalators to try to land on the 'Up escalator'.

Sidebottom hadn't thought this latest plan through though. He had just been sprinting in the opposite direction to the escalator but now when he landed he was still sprinting very hard but this time it was in the same direction as the 'Up escalator'.

"No Sidebottom!!" I yelled. It was too late. Sidebottom went flying forwards and crashed into all the people in front of him.

First he crashed into a lady carrying a huge cream cake. She let go of the cake and it went flying high up into the air.

That woman then crashed into a man who was drinking a bottle of water, who coated himself and the lady with water.

That man then clattered into another woman who was carrying an apple pie which then splatted into the face of a man who had turned round to see what was going on.

At about this time, the big cake that had flown high into the air had started coming back down to earth.

Sidebottom meanwhile had landed on his backside and was just sitting up trying to work out what had just happened.

"Sidebottom - watch out for the cake!" I shouted as I watched the cake heading down towards the escalator. Just at that moment Sidebottom looked upwards.

SPLAT!!! Straight in his face. It then rolled down onto the rest of him covering him from head to toe in cream and chocolate. He wiped the cream away from his eyes so he could see.

I walked up the escalator towards him and handed him a cloth to wipe his face, then I helped up the other customers who were all muttering at Sidebottom.

"Imbecile." One man said

"Dunderhead," said the woman.

"Come on, Mr Langley," said Sidebottom, seemingly oblivious to the comments of the other customers, "I want to try on some costumes." Sidebottom then ran up the escalator and disappeared into one of the clothes areas. I slowly trudged after him.

When I caught up with him a couple of minutes later there were superhero costumes all over the floor. I looked at the mess of clothes everywhere, many of which seemed torn and ripped.

"Sidebottom! What are you doing?" I said as I watched in disbelief as

Sidebottom tried to pull on a children's Iron Man costume. "Sidebottom, that's a children's costume. You're an adult!" Just as I had finished speaking, Sidebottom pulled the small Iron Man trousers up.

"RRRRIIIPPP." The Iron Man costume tore in half.

"Ah!" said Sidebottom. "I wonder if that's why they don't fit, Mr Langley."

"You clot, Sidebottom!" I started picking up the clothes from the floor. "Right, stop trying on clothes. We need to go."

"Why do we need to go?"

"Because you've just destroyed half the store!" I exclaimed. "Plus I've just had a text from that buffoon, McPlop. He's decided to turn up at the supermarket as well and he's down at the counter buying chocolate."

I made my way towards the escalator to go down to the counter to find McPlop. Sure enough I could see him in his football kit. He turned around and had, what appeared to be, seven chocolate bars sticking out of his mouth."

"McPlop! What are you doing?" I said as I wandered up to him. "Have you paid for those chocolate bars?"

"Uggurddrpplnnn" said McPlop, who was unable to talk properly due to having so many chocolate bars in his mouth.

"What?" I asked.

"Iveguurrraplannn," repeated McPlop.

"I have absolutely no idea what you're saying, McPlop. Here's an idea, why don't you take the seven chocolate bars out of your mouth and then I might be able to understand what on earth you are banging on about." McPlop kept on eating the chocolate until he could finally speak again.

"I said, 'I have a plan'." McPlop explained. "If I eat all the chocolate bars before I get to the counter, I won't have to pay for them."

"Yep brilliant, McPlop. Well done." I said sarcastically.

I looked around to see Sidebottom

walking towards us. He was wearing what appeared to be a children's Hulk outfit which was clearly too small for him but he had somehow managed to squeeze into.

"It fits, Mr Langley!" said Sidebottom beaming.

"Brilliant, Sidebottom. You've surpassed yourself once more." I turned back round. "For goodness sake, I'm going to have to pay for all of this."

"No. Allow me," said McPlop as he handed the seven empty chocolate wrappers to the woman behind the till. The woman looked at McPlop in bemusement. "We'll take that Hulk costume as well," said McPlop pointing at Sidebottom, who looked frankly ridiculous. The woman tapped some numbers into her till.

"That'll be twenty pounds. How do you want to pay?" McPlop turned to the little shelf that held the chocolate bars behind him. Hoping nobody would notice, he tore a small rectangle of cardboard from the little sign attached to the chocolate stand.

"I'll pay by card please," replied McPlop. The woman, who hadn't seen what McPlop was up to, held the card machine out for McPlop. "Beep," said McPlop, as he swiped his bit of cardboard over the card machine.

"McPlop, what on earth are you doing?" I said exasperated. McPlop winked at me.

"I've just paid, Mr Langley."

"No, McPlop, you haven't just paid. You have just waved a piece of cardboard over the card reader and said the word 'beep' out loud." I pulled out twenty pounds from my wallet. "Here you go." I said to the poor woman behind the till. "Right you two cretins. Home, now!"

# The Warehouse Fire

I was fast asleep in bed in the early hours of a Wednesday morning when I heard a fire engine not far from my house. It woke me from my slumber and I looked out of the window to see what was going on. To my surprise the old disused warehouse, which was about a hundred metres from my house, was a mass of orange flames as it burnt and lit up the darkness.

"Wow," I said out loud. I hadn't seen anything quite as spectacular as this for a while. I watched another fire engine arrive at the scene and I could see some figures walking towards the burning building. I decided to dress and go over there to see if I could help at all.

A few minutes later I was crossing the road and wandering over the grass verge in my jeans and sweater. It was summertime and so was very mild. I carried a couple of buckets of water with me. I didn't think it would help the firemen much but felt I should make an effort of some kind.

As I approached the fire, which was getting larger as it spread throughout the warehouse, I recognised someone who was standing watching the firemen do their work.

"Sidebottom," I said, "what are you doing here?" I put the two buckets on the ground.

"Watching the fire, Mr Langley. There was nothing on television so I thought I would come and watch this instead."

"Sidebottom, are you in your pyjamas?" I looked him up and down.

"Of course, I've even got my slippers on," he said wiggling his slippers in my direction. I shook my head in disbelief. Sidebottom then moved over to, what looked like, an old abandoned sofa that was to his right and plumped down into it.

"Hang on. Where did that sofa come from, Sidebottom?"

"It's mine, Mr Langley. I wheeled it

over from my house. I wanted a comfy seat whilst I watched the fire. Best seat in the house!"

"Unbelievable." I replied.

At that moment I noticed a small table in front of Sidebottom's sofa with some items on it. Sidebottom picked up a mug from the table and started slurping out of it.

"I brought my cafetiere too," Sidebottom explained, "it's times like this that you can't beat having a good frappuccino."

I had almost lost the will to live by this point, when someone wandered up beside me.

"Ah, McPlop," I said, as I turned to look at the new arrival, "hopefully you'll bring some sanity to proceedings. Lord knows, I can't get any from Sidebottom."

"Morning, McPlop." Sidebottom said, "Fancy a frappuccino?"

"Don't rise to it, McPlop." I said, looking at McPlop. "You'll only encourage him."

"Don't mind if I do," said McPlop, quite excited at having a Frapaccino in the dark. He wandered past me and plonked himself down next to Sidebottom.

I looked at what McPlop was wearing. It seemed to be an outfit with teddy bears on it.

"Pyjamas. You as well?" I rolled my eyes. "Am I the only one who's sane here?"

One of the firemen glanced around and saw the pair sitting on the sofa, dressed in their pyjamas, slurping their drinks. He looked bemused and then went back to spraying the huge fire with a jet of water from the fire engine.

"Would you like a beer, Mr Langley?"

"What?"

"A beer."

"Where would you get a beer from at two o'clock in the morning in the middle of a field?"

"From my mini-fridge," answered Sidebottom enthusiastically.

"What mini-fridge?" I asked.

Sidebottom leaned down and opened the door of a mini-fridge which was by his feet.

"You brought a mini-fridge with you?" I said increduously. "You'll be telling me next that you brought popcorn."

Sidebottom opened a carrier bag that was wedged between him and McPlop, pulled out a packet and held it up.

"Popcorn." I said, looking at the package. "Brilliant, Sidebottom." I continued sarcastically. "Award winning."

"Thanks." Sidebottom beamed a smile, totally oblivious to the sarcasm in my voice.

"Sidebottom, are you aware there is a building on fire just there in front of you?" I pointed at the blazing warehouse with its huge flames. Orange cinders were flicking up into the air like fire-flies. "Could you not have brought some buckets of water to throw on the fire to at least help the firemen." I pointed at the buckets I had brought that were still beside me on the ground.

"But if I carried buckets of water, I would've had to leave the cafetiere behind?" Sidebottom replied, looking horrified and completely flummoxed by the whole concept.

"Nice frappuccino this, Sidebottom," McPlop said suddenly.

"Ah, McPlop. Good of you to join the conversation." I said turning to McPlop.

"You don't have one of those chocolate shakers that they have in the coffee shops, do you?" McPlop asked Sidebottom. "You know the ones; where they sprinkle chocolate powder on in the shape of a snowflake"

"No he doesn't!" I exclaimed.

"That's not quite true, Mr Langley." Sidebottom reached into his bag again. "Funny you should ask, McPlop." He pulled out a chocolate shaker that he had obviously pinched from the local coffee shop judging by the writing on the side of it. "It's not in the shape of a snowflake but would a palm tree do, McPlop?"

"Certainly would!" said McPlop,

happily.

"Right! That's me done!" I said. "I'm going to leave you two clowns to your refreshments." I picked up the two buckets to set off to help the fireman.

"Are you sure I can't interest you in an 'iced skinny latte'?" Shouted Sidebottom after me, as he shook his cafetiere encouragingly.

"No, I certainly don't want an 'iced skinny latte', Sidebottom." I replied.

"Ah, you must be a 'skinny caramel frappe', type of person then?" Sidebottom shouted after me.

"No, I'm not." I shouted back, and then stopped and turned round. "But, do you know what? I'm going to throw these buckets of water on the fire and then when I return I want you to make me a 'mocha frappe magical unicorn latte with fresh dinosaur milk'. Is that ok?"

Sidebottom looked a bit confused. He then looked inside his cafetiere.

"Yes, I should be able to rustle up one of those, Mr Langley."

"Right.  I'm out of here."  I said as I wandered off towards the firemen.

# McPlop and the Sat Nav

"How's your leg, Mr Langley?" McPlop asked me as I climbed gingerly into the passenger seat of my car after the end of the football match he and I had been playing in.

"Sore, McPlop. That was a nasty tackle from their central defender. I'm going to struggle to drive us home."

"No problem. I can drive your car, Mr Langley. I'm a great driver." McPlop beamed at me as he climbed into the driver's seat.

He then pressed the button to start the car and the engine roared into life. I buckled up.

"Do you mind if I try out my new sat nav, Mr Langley?" McPlop pulled a little black box, a wire and holder out of his kit bag. "I've just purchased it from the interweb."

"InterNET, McPlop!"

"Yeah, that's the fella." I shook my

head in resignation.

McPlop then licked his spit onto the big sucker section on the bottom of the sat nav holder and with saliva dripping off it, stamped it onto my spotless dashboard and moved it around spreading his saliva all over.

"For goodness sake McPlop, you idiot! I've now got your spit all over my dashboard. That's disgusting."

"Ah, sorry, Mr Langley. Do you want me to move it somewhere else?"

"No! It's done now." I shook my head. "Honestly, it's like dealing with Sidebottom." I frowned. "Speaking of which, where is Sidebottom these days? I haven't seen that buffoon for ages."

"Apparently he's been doing something top secret."

"Top secret? Oh cripes, what's he up to now?" I groaned.

"Not sure, but he's been auditioning for it. He's keeping it very hush-hush and says that I will find out soon." McPlop jabbed at couple of buttons on the sat nav.

"I programmed the 'Home' button earlier to my address." He pressed the home button and the sat nav stirred into action.

"It's an obscure make of sat nav, this one McPlop, I've never heard of it." I squinted at the odd name.

"Sidebottom advised me to get it. He said it was the greatest sat nav in the whole world." McPlop released the hand brake, pressed the accelerator and set off from the football club car park.

"Hmmm," I raised an eyebrow. "Guaranteed disaster."

We pulled out onto the main road and quickly sped up until McPlop levelled off at about fifty miles an hour. McPlop turned the volume up on his sat nav and suddenly it sparked into life.

*"Hello! This is your sat nav speaking."*

"That voice sounds familiar," I commented.

*"Set off,"* the sat nav instructed.

"We have set off." I muttered.

*"Set off now,"*

"We have set off you stupid sat nav," I

mumbled.  "That voice sounds really familiar. I just can't quite place it."  I said, scratching my chin.

*"Congratulations, you have now set off."*

"I do know that voice," I groaned, "I know exactly who it is."  My shoulders slumped. "It's that idiot Sidebottom. That's what he must have been doing all this time...working for a sat nav company where they recorded his voice doing directions.  No wonder he wanted you to buy this make of sat nav."

*"Turn left ahead,"* said the Sidebottom voice. *"Turn left now."*

"It sounds like Sidebottom must know a short cut."

McPlop flicked the indicator on and swerved the car down the road to the left. The road was a winding one and fairly narrow.

"Does this feel like we're going in the right direction to you, McPlop?" I was doubtful.

"I'm rubbish at directions, Mr Langley but these sat navs are great."  McPlop continued a couple of miles down the road until we approached a large clearing with a house and a road on the right that lead to a huge duck pond.

"*Turn right ahead,*" said the sat nav.

"What?" I said, surprised. "Going right would take us into the duck pond. There's no other right turn."

"*Take the next turn on the right,*" said the Sidebottom voice.

"McPlop...don't do it." I said sternly. "It's a duck pond."

"But it's telling me to go that way," reasoned McPlop.

"Ignore it you fool." I instructed him.

"But the sat nav, Mr Langley?"

"It's a duck pond, McPlop."

McPlop turned a sharp right.

"Not the duck pond McPlop!" I shouted.

"*Turn right into the duck pond.*" said the sat nav.

"Nooo, McPlop." I yelled. "Don't listen to that idiot Sidebottom!"

The car went straight in to the water

with a huge splash.

"You imbecile, McPlop!"

The bonnet of the car started disappearing under the water. "Aaargh, get out of the car!" I shouted.

"The door's jammed, Mr Langley," yelled McPlop, who was now beginning to cry.

"Stop crying McPlop for goodness sake, it's only a duck pond. Just push your door harder."

A few minutes later I was sitting next to McPlop on the bank of the duck pond. I had pulled my football boots off which were soaked through and was in the process of wringing my socks out. I shook my head at him.

"Dullard." I muttered, as I looked at my new car that was half way into the duck pond.

"Sorry, Mr Langley." McPlop tipped one of his boots upside down and water poured out. "How long did the car recovery man say he'd be?"

"Twenty minutes." I rattled my watch,

which had got soaked as well. "Rats, my watch has stopped working."

The recovery truck arrived on time and began the slow process of towing my car out of the duck pond. After an inspection of the car the recovery man walked over to where we were sitting.

"You're very lucky," he said, wiping his hands on an old rag, "the engine's in tact. Any deeper in the water and it could have been very expensive. I've started her up and she seems to be running fine. I would avoid driving into any more duck ponds though." He grinned.

"Are you taking notes on what this man is saying, McPlop." I said shaking my head.

"That'll be a hundred pounds," said the recovery man.

"A hundred pounds!" I exclaimed.

"I can let the car roll back into the duck pond if it's too much money," suggested the car recovery man.

"Alright, alright." I pulled some notes out of my wallet and handed the money over to the man. "It was a good thing I had plenty of cash with me."

McPlop and I climbed into the car which was still soaked with water but had the engine running.

"A hundred pounds," I sighed. "Right, if the car's working. Let's go home."

McPlop started the car again and we set off. We decided to continue along the road we had come down. It was a long straight road and we could see a mile or so into the distance. There were no turn offs, just fields on both sides.

"*Keep going straight. Do not turn off,*" said the sat nav.

"Brilliant." I said. "It managed to work that out on its own."

A few minutes later the weather started getting worse, the clouds darkened and the rain came down, bouncing off the car roof and bonnet.

"*Turn right in one hundred metres,*" instructed the Sidebottom voice.

"What?" I said. "There's no turning for

a mile, never mind a hundred metres. McPlop, this Sidebottom sat nav is useless." I moaned.

*"Turn right in fifty metres,"* said the sat nav as we motored along.

"Maybe we should do what it says," suggested McPlop.

"McPlop, we are not driving off this road into the middle of a muddy field," I said sternly, "Do I make myself clear?"

*"Turn right into the muddy field,"* said the sat nav.

"McPlop don't do it." I said firmly.

"But the sat nav, Mr Langley!" reasoned McPlop.

"McPlop," I said very patiently, "we've discussed this. Can you remember what happened last time?"

"The duck pond, Mr Langley."

"That's right, McPlop. You drove into a duck pond."

*"Turn right into the muddy field now,"* ordered the sat nav.

"McPlop, that field has cows in it, which means it will be full of cow pats. If you drive into that field you'll be pushing the car out on your own, do you understand?"

*"Turn right into the field full of cow pats,"* said the Sidebottom voice.

"It really wants me to turn into the field though, Mr Langley!"

McPlop swerved to the right.

"Nooo, McPlop you idiot!" The car zoomed off the road, "Not the cow pats!" I shouted as we careered down the banking and splatted into the muddy field. The aroma of cow pats that we had landed in, wafted in through the open car window.

"You imbecile, McPlop!"

Twenty minutes later McPlop and I stood on the banking watching the car recovery man reverse his truck backwards to pull my car out of the field.

"Busy day for you boys," chuckled the recovery man. "That'll be another hundred pounds please," he said, as he leant his head out of the window of his truck.

I whacked McPlop over the head with my wallet and handed the cash over to the recovery man.

"Right we need to turn this sat nav off, McPlop, it's a disaster."

"I've no idea where we are though, Mr Langley." I looked all around. He was right. I had no idea where we were either and the recovery man had driven off. "We have to keep it on."

"Right." I groaned. "This voice of Sidebottom's is really annoying me though," I said to McPlop as we climbed back into the car, "can we change it to something else?"

As we were still parked, McPlop thought it a sensible idea to give my suggestion a try. He started furiously pressing buttons on the sat nav. I watched him as he whacked button after button for about fifteen seconds.

"McPlop, you have absolutely no idea what you're doing, do you?"

"I've almost got it, Mr Langley." He replied as he hacked away at one particular button.

"*Language change*," announced the sat nav. "*Bonjour! C'est your new sat nav a la francais speaking.*"

"Oh, brilliant McPlop, it's still that idiot Sidebottom talking but now he's trying to talk in French."

"But I can't speak or understand French, Mr Langley?"

"Clearly neither can Sidebottom," I replied.

"This sat nav isn't going to be much use getting us home now, Mr Langley."

"It wasn't much use getting us home before." I pointed out. "Now it's still useless, but it's useless in French instead. And I use the word 'French' in the loosest sense of the term." I pointed at the sat nav. "How about you whack some more buttons." I suggested.

McPlop obliged.

"*Language change*," announced the sat nav. "*Willkommen.*"

"What language is that Mr Langley?" asked a confused McPlop.

"You've changed it from French to German somehow. 'Willkommen' means 'Welcome'." I replied. McPlop angrily punched another couple of buttons.

*"McPlop ist ein kompletter idiot."* The Sidebottom sat nav said in German.

"Ha." I laughed. Even I could translate that and I didn't know any German. "Maybe the sat nav isn't so stupid after all." I grinned. McPlop still had no idea what was being said.

"How about you work your magic again on it, McPlop." I suggested.

"Gladly," said McPlop, who this time unclipped the sat nav from its holder, head butted it and then put it back in the holder."

"Ingenious, McPlop. You should work in computing with skills like those..." I said sarcastically, before I was interrupted by the sat nav again.

*"Language change."* It announced. *"Hello! This is your sat nav speaking."*

"Incredible McPlop, I was wrong. It turns out you're actually a computing genius. It's now back to Sidebottom speaking in English. Right, lets go before he starts speaking in Outer Mongolian."

After about fifteen minutes driving we seemed to at last be heading in roughly the right direction.

"I recognise this road, this is now the way we came." I sighed with relief. "Hopefully we'll get home soon."

*"Take a short cut home by taking the road on the right,"* said the Sidebottom voice.

"Interesting. I've not been down that road. Looks a bit narrow." I pondered.

"Let's take it," shouted McPlop and swerved across the road which had oncoming traffic flying towards us.

"Aargh! I didn't mean take the road McPlop, I was just wondering about it!" It was too late now though. We had cut across the busy road and now entered the narrow road on the right. "What was that sign back there, McPlop. Did you see it?"

I was sure there was an important sign that we had driven past. "This is a very thin road, it's only one car width." I frowned as I looked at the signs ahead. "Wait, those signs are facing the wrong way. We can only see the back of them."

"Maybe they put them all back to front on this road," McPlop suggested.

"You imbecile, McPlop! When do they ever put signs back to front? You do realise what this means, don't you?" I yelled. "We're going the wrong way down a one-way street!" McPlop was still flooring the accelerator and suddenly a car appeared ahead of us rocketing in our direction at high speed.

*"Turn around where possible."* The sat nav said calmly.

"Turn around where possible?!" I exclaimed. "How on earth can we turn around you stupid sat nav, it's a one way street!"

*"Turn around where possible."* It repeated. *"You are driving the wrong way down a one way street."*

"Aargh, you told us to come down here you clueless hunk of junk!" I shouted at the little machine attached to the dashboard. "Brake McPlop!" I yelled. "McPlop slammed his foot on the brake and the car came to a shuddering halt only a couple of metres from the oncoming car which had also hit its brakes.

After a moment's silence, where we could see the faces of the shocked people in the car in front of us, we could hear a police siren. It was getting louder. I looked behind me through the back window.

"Oh great," I groaned as I saw the flashing blue lights of a police van pull up behind us.

A few minutes later McPlop and I were sitting on the banking next to the road being given a lecture by a policeman.

"The law has changed recently," explained the policeman, "any car spotted driving the wrong way down a one-way street, gets an on-the-spot fine of a hundred pounds."

"Of course they do." I said.

"I don't have any money, Mr Langley," said a sheepish, McPlop.

"Of course you don't." I said, unsurprised.

"Here," I chucked my wallet at the policeman, "keep it."

The policeman looked inside the wallet, extracted the last hundred pounds and then handed it back to me.

"Three hundred quid, McPlop. That's what it's cost me today. Quite an achievement considering that you've only actually been driving the car for about twenty minutes. It's a good job we haven't got another hour ahead of us or I'd be bankrupt." I wandered back over to the car, leaned in through the window and plucked the sat nav from the dashboard.

*"Turn around where possible,"* said the Sidebottom sat nav. *"Do not go the wrong way down one way streets."* It helpfullly advised.

"Shut up Sidebottom, you blithering idiot!" I yelled at the little machine that was in my hand. I dropped it on the floor and started jumping up and down on it like a mad man.

"Take this" I shouted as I crashed my foot down on to it.

*"Turn around where..."* I stamped my foot down harder.

*"..pffubull,"* said the sat nav in a broken voice. All the bits were smashed everywhere. McPlop ran over and started joining me jumping up and down on every bit of the machine that was left.

"Idiot Sidebottom!" we both shouted as we stamped up and down with joy.

# Sidebottom and McPlop try Karate

It was a warm summer's day and I was finishing painting the front door of my house when I heard a cough behind me. I put the paint brush down into the tin of red paint that was by my feet and turned around to see who was visiting.

"Morning, Mr Langley!" said Sidebottom and McPlop in unison.

I shielded my eyes from the sun as I looked at the pair of them, then stood up and stretched my legs out which had been stiff from crouching for so long.

"You two look very pleased with yourselves." I paused as I looked at what they were wearing. "Two questions though. Why are you dressed like that and why have you both got bare feet?" I said, puzzled.

McPlop and Sidebottom looked at each other's costumes which were all white with both wearing belts.

"We're Karate experts, Mr Langley." Sidebottom said triumphantly. "These are white Karate outfits. My name is 'Sensei Sidebottom' and this is my assistant, 'Kung Fu McPlop'. 'Sensei' means 'teacher' in Japanese," Sidebottom explained.

"Sidebottom, those are not Karate outfits that you're wearing."

"Yes, definitely Karate outfits, Mr Langley."

"Sidebottom, you and McPlop are clearly both wearing white bathrobes. They're all fluffy for a start. Proper Karate outfits aren't fluffy," I noticed some writing on the bottom of his bath robe, "plus it says 'Hotel property' on the bottom of both those robes." I thought about it for a second. "Have you pinched those bathrobes from a hotel, Sidebottom?"

"Um, no definitely not, Mr Langley," said Sidebottom, coughing slightly as he spoke.

"What does that other piece of writing say?" I squinted at it to get a better look. "It says 'Hotel Property - DO NOT REMOVE'." I shook my head, "Sidebottom you clot, you've clearly swiped those bathrobes from a Hotel."

"Um, anyway, Mr Langley," Sidebottom said, changing the subject, " I just came to tell you that I, Sensei Sidebottom, and my faithful sidekick, Kung Fu McPlop, are going to the local Karate centre to teach people the ancient art of Karate." Sidebottom nodded in acknowledgement of how wise he thought he sounded.

"But neither of you know how to do Karate," I pointed out. "If you were going to teach people how to steal fluffy bath robes and wander around the streets in bare feet, then you two would be experts, but I don't think there's too much demand for learning that."

"That's where you're wrong, Mr Langley." Sidebottom beamed. "Both myself and Kung Fu McPlop here, have been doing training all morning on

Karate."

"What type of training," I asked, narrowing my eyes at him.

"Well, we watched a movie called 'The Karate Kid'."

"Brilliant." I said. "Any training other than that?"

"No, that's pretty much it."

"Yep. Thought as much." I shook my head in despair.

Sidebottom then thought of something. "Why don't you come along and see us in action, Mr Langley? It'll be great. You'll get to see us doing Karate-chops on people. Like this!" Sidebottom turned round to McPlop, who was paying no attention at all, and Karate-chopped him in the peanuts.

"Oooo!" said McPlop as he crumpled to the floor in pain, "Right in the goolies." He moaned.

"Do you know what?" I said, "I would love to come. I suspect it will be quite entertaining seeing you two clowns in action." I looked at McPlop who was now doing a premier-league roll on the floor. "McPlop, get up!" I said.

I put my brush and tin of paint inside the garage, pulled the garage door down and then locked my front door.

"Right, where's this Karate centre?"

"This way, Mr Langley! Follow me! I'll be able to show you what a tough martial arts master I am."

As soon as we walked out of my smooth driveway though we got to the pavement which had a loose stony surface. Sensei Sidebottom and Kung Fu McPlop were still in bare feet.

"Ow, ouch, ouch, ouch," yelped Sidebottom as he tried to tip toe along the path. After a minute or so, Sidebottom reached into the pockets of his bathrobe and pulled out a pair of slippers. Not just any slippers though, these were pink fluffy slippers.

"It's no use, it's too stony. I'll have to wear slippers," concluded Sidebottom as he dropped his slippers to the ground and stepped into them. McPlop looked at

Sidebottom's pink fluffy slippers and started laughing.

"I thought you were a 'tough martial arts master', Sidebottom." McPlop chuckled. "My granny has pink slippers like those."

"I am a tough martial arts master!" Sidebottom said indignantly.

We carried on walking for a bit. McPlop was trying to suppress his giggles.

"Psst, Sidebottom," whispered McPlop out of the side of his mouth, "my granny's just rung and she says she wants her fluffy slippers back," McPlop said, and burst into laughter at the hilarity of his own joke.

"Shut up, McPlop," said Sidebottom, "unless you want another Karate chop in the peanuts."

"Pah, bring it on, Sidebottom." I have iron peanuts that can easily withstand another one of your attacks."

"Enough!" I shouted. "Less talking, more walking, the pair of you! And make sure you both walk ten metres in front of me. I don't want to get spotted being seen with you two clowns."

After ten minutes walking, which drew some strange looks from passers-by, we eventually came to the local village hall.

"This is it, Mr Langley." Sidebottom announced. "This is where the instructor told us to come to help him with his Karate lessons."

We opened the door to the village hall and turned into the main hall where there was a Karate lesson underway with a teacher and a large group of eight year olds.

"You might want to put your slippers away now Sidebottom, seeing as everyone else is in barefeet." I advised. Sidebottom hastily grabbed them and stuffed the slippers back into his pockets.

Just then the Karate instructor spotted the three of us.

"Ah! Now children," he said, addressing his class, "we have two men here who have told me they are Karate experts. They have come to give you a demonstration and some advice. I need to carry out some administrative work, so I will leave you in their capable hands." He looked over at Sidebottom and McPlop, "Gentlemen, they are all yours." With that, he swept out of the hall into a side room.

"Good morning children," said Sidebottom as he walked across the room to where they were. McPlop trotted after him. "My name is 'Sensei Sidebottom' and this is my completely useless assistant, 'Kung Fu McPlop'." Some of the children laughed.

"Some of you may have seen the film called, 'The Karate Kid'. Well, children, let me tell you, I am like the wise old Karate expert in that film. I am so powerful at Karate that I could render McPlop unconscious with one swift Karate chop, using just my little finger."

"Rubbish," said McPlop under his breath.

"Silence, my useless assistant," instructed Sidebottom.

One of the children put his hand up.

"Yes little boy, what is it?" asked Sensei Sidebottom.

"Why are you wearing a fluffy white bath robe if you're a Karate expert?"

"Don't you start!" said Sidebottom.

"And why have you got fluffy pink slippers sticking out of your pockets?" asked another child.

Sidebottom stuffed them further down into his pockets.

"Those are like my granny's slippers," remarked another boy.

"Enough!" said Sidebottom. "Now my assistant, Kung Fu McPlop, will do a Karate demonstration for you. Then I will demonstrate to you the ancient art of 'surprise'."

All of a sudden McPlop started doing all kinds of bizarre Karate actions. His hands and legs were shooting out in every direction. Neither myself, Sidebottom or the children had ever seen any of these moves before. It looked very much like he was making them up as he was going along. After a few minutes McPlop was starting to sweat and get very tired. The kids were all looking at him, rather bemused.

"Now children, for the art of surprise." Sidebottom said. He then did a huge Karate chop right between McPlop's legs.

"Ooooooo," said McPlop as he crumpled to the floor. "Right in the peanuts," he moaned.

"Now that, is the element of surprise, children," said Sidebottom.

McPlop did a premier league roll from where the kids were, right across to my feet and then rolled all the way back again.

"Get up McPlop," said Sidebottom. "Now children, who would like to take on my assistant at a Karate fight?"

"Me, me, me!" shouted a number of the kids.

Sidebottom surveyed all the hands that were in the air. He plumped for the biggest boy in the group.

"You boy. Come up here and prepare for battle against the mighty Kung Fu

McPlop!"

McPlop, who had now recovered and was just about standing, started shooting his arms and legs out in some attempt at Karate moves. The child who had volunteered, stood watching him.

"Hee ya!" shouted McPlop as he chopped his hand through the air, nowhere near the child. "Look how powerful I am. Haaaa ya!" He shouted again with a Karate kick that completely missed the child. In fact the boy was just standing exactly where he was with his arms folded, looking very unimpressed.

"Your bath robe's come undone!" Shouted one of the children in the group.

"I can see his pants!" Yelled another and started laughing.

McPlop immediately looked down to see if his pants were on show.

Just then, the child he was supposed to be fighting, saw his opportunity and ran forward as fast as he could. He launched himself into the air with his leg flying out in front of him and shot a Karate kick straight into McPlop's goolies.

"Ooooooooo," groaned McPlop as he crumpled to the floor.

Just then the instructor came back into the room. The instructor was a '3rd Dan' black belt which meant not only was he a black belt, which is the best level in Karate, he was a '3rd Dan' which meant he was a brilliant black belt. He looked at McPlop who was blubbering on the floor.

"For goodness sakes man, stop crying." The instructor said. He then noticed Sidebottom and McPlop's fluffy white bathrobes. "Hang on a minute, what are you two wearing?"

"This is a Karate outfit. Look..." Sidebottom was pointing at his belt, "I've got a black belt like you."

"No, you're wearing a fluffy bath robe and that belt says 'Marks and Spencer's' on it. Earning a black belt takes years of Karate training. You two clowns have just been to Marks and Spencers and bought a couple of trouser belts and are pretending you're Karate instructors."

"Fight!" shouted one of the children.

"Fight," shouted another.

"Fight, fight, fight..." the children chanted.

"Good idea children," said the instructor, "it's time for you two buffoons to have a proper Karate fight; against each other."

"Bring it on!" shouted McPlop, getting all pumped up.

"Come and get it!" responded Sidebottom, dancing around like a boxer.

"Come on then!" McPlop retorted, doing a fancy shuffle with his feet and waving his hands around.

"Yeah, come on then, McPlop, if you think you're hard enough."

"Definitely hard enough to beat you."

Both men were dancing around but neither was even attempting to fight at all. The instructor moved towards them.

"Start fighting!" he said. "The loser fights me."

Sidebottom and McPlop suddenly looked very worried. Both decided to attack instantly. The pair launched Karate kicks at each other at exactly the same second and both caught the other square in the goolies.

"Ooooooo," they both moaned as the pair slumped to the floor, clutching their nether regions.

"Unbelievable," muttered the instructor.

Sidebottom and McPlop were both on the floor weeping.

"Stop wining, the pair of you. Honestly, you're grown men. Now get up."

Sidebottom and McPlop stopped wining and stood up gingerly. Sidebottom recovered a little quicker.

"Do you know what level of black belt I am?" asked the instructor to Sidebottom.

"Um, dark black?" suggested Sidebottom.

"Imbecile!" The instructor said and clipped Sidebottom round his head. "I'm a 3rd Dan."

"Oh right," said Sidebottom, "But if you're a 3rd Dan, where are the first two

Dan's?" Sidebottom looked around the room searching for another couple of people called Dan.

"What? Right, that's it! I've had enough of you two prats. Get out of my Karate school before I set my eight year olds on you!"

The eight year olds all got up and stood in fight pose. Sidebottom and McPlop took one look at them and turned and fled out of the hall. "Run for your life, Mr Langley." They shouted as they zoomed past me.

I grinned at the instructor who gave me a wave and I followed the two idiots out of the village hall, and watched them as they ran off into the distance.

# McPlop takes to the skies

I was weeding the flower bed in my front garden one glorious day when I saw McPlop coming into view. I ducked behind a nearby tree to try and avoid him. McPlop walked along the path in front of my house and stopped and looked at my house, clearly trying to work out if I was in. He then looked all around the garden.

"I'm not going to get away with this." I muttered to myself as I tried to move even further out of sight. McPlop was looking everywhere.

"Good morning, Mr Langley." He said, cheerily as he finally spotted me. "What are you doing behind that tree?"

My shoulders slumped.

"Ah, McPlop. I didn't see you there," I fibbed. "I'm just...um...cutting these branches back."

"I have some very exciting news."

"Go on," I said, resigned to no doubt more rubbish.

"Well, as you know, I'm an estate agent by trade but for the last few years I have been training as an airline pilot in my spare time."

"Really?" I said. "That's actually quite impressive, McPlop." I said raising my eyebrows.

"Look, here's my certificate, I've passed the pilot exams!"

I examined the piece of paper. Sure enough, McPlop was a qualified airline pilot.

"Well done, McPlop."

"I fly my first jumbo jet today from Leeds-Bradford Airport to Gran Canaria. There's even a perk, I've been given one free airline ticket, so I've given it to Sidebottom as I've got an extra special surprise for him. McPlop winked at me.

Just then, Sidebottom himself wandered up with a huge amount of luggage. He was wheeling two bright purple suitcases, a yellow rucksack and a brown shopping bag with him.

"Very colour co-ordinated there I see,

Sidebottom." I said sarcastically.

I frowned as I looked at all the luggage.

"How long are you going away for?"

"Four days," replied Sidebottom.

"You're only going away for four days? Surely you don't need all that luggage then?"

"I've just packed a few essentials, Mr Langley."

"Such as?"

"Lots of pants. Tons of them. You can never be too careful. Imagine if I went on holiday and hadn't packed enough pants, Mr Langley."

"Surely you don't need that many pairs of pants when you're only going away for four days?"

"You can never have too many pants in my experience, Mr Langley."

"Right, time to leave Sidebottom." McPlop said. "I've got a plane to fly!"

An hour later the pair had arrived in the departure lounge at Leeds-Bradford airport.

"I have to get changed into my pilot's uniform, Sidebottom," said McPlop smugly.

"And I have to check-in my luggage," responded his companion.

At the check-in desk Sidebottom decided to send all his luggage to be put into the cargo hold on the aeroplane.

About an hour later he had passed through customs and was walking through the tunnel that took him directly to the plane.

Through a window in the tunnel Sidebottom could see McPlop sitting in the pilot's seat, dressed in his pilot's uniform, doing some last minute checks. McPlop turned at that moment and saw Sidebottom.

"Hi, McPlop," mouthed Sidebottom waving his free airline ticket at McPlop. The pilot gave him a wave of acknowledgement from the aeroplane cabin.

Sidebottom reached the aeroplane and boarded, giving the stewardesses a big smile.

Meanwhile in the cabin, McPlop turned around to see Sidebottom searching for his seat.

"Time for some revenge," sniggered McPlop to himself.

After making sure Sidebottom was comfortable in his seat, the stewardess returned to the cabin and McPlop had a quick word with her.

"Ellen, I want you to serve that man there," he pointed at Sidebottom, "as much gravy on his lunch as possible. Make it nice and hot too."

"Yes, sir" she replied, a little confused.

After another ten minutes the seat belt signs went on and the plane taxied along the runway. McPlop pulled back the throttle on the plane and the huge Boeing 737 rocketed down the runway and soared into the sky. After fifteen minutes the stewardess started serving the meals. Having given Sidebottom his extra hot lunch with extra super-hot gravy, she returned to the cabin.

"I've served that man his lunch with extra gravy, just as you ordered Pilot McPlop."

"Good work, Ellen. Now go and sit down and strap yourself in."

"Yes, sir." She did as she was told.

McPlop then pulled back on the stick and the big jumbo jet lurched upwards at a rapid rate. All the passengers were able to hold onto their lunch trays except Sidebottom whose large amount of gravy tipped all over him

"Aaarghh, I'm burning, I'm burning. My pants are burning," shouted Sidebottom as he tried to brush the gravy off but only succeeded in spreading it everywhere, "Aaargh, it's soaked through my trousers. Aarrgh it's burning my peanuts," he yelled. "It's burning the peanuts!"

"Get that man some water," shouted McPlop from the cabin. McPlop levelled off the plane.

Ellen the stewardess ran down the plane with a big jug of water. However as she ran up to Sidebottom she accidentally tripped over another passenger's outstretched leg and and the whole jug of water went all over Sidebottom.

SPLASH. She completely covered him.

"Pfft, pfft," said Sidebottom spitting water out of his mouth and wiping his face. "You stupid idiot," he shouted, "I'm going to have to go to the toilet, to clean all this gravy off and dry myself now." Sidebottom walked up the plane towards the toilets with the other passengers chuckling.

Once he reached the plane toilet he locked himself in and started taking off some of his wet clothes.

"Time for a wee too," he muttered. He started whistling loudly as he tried to wee whilst standing up in a moving plane. "Balancing is tricky," he muttered to himself.

Meanwhile the stewardess returned to the cabin.

"Good work." McPlop chuckled. "Where is he now?"

"He's just gone to the toilet."

"Really?" said McPlop, his ears pricking up with the news, "I don't suppose you heard him whistling did you?"

"Funnily enough, yes, he's got a loud whistle, I could hear him through the door as I passed by."

"Ha, brilliant. Sidebottom always whistles when he's having a wee. Ellen, go and strap yourself in again."

"Yes, Pilot McPlop."

McPlop then lowered the elevators causing the aeroplane's nose to drop. The plane lurched downwards.

Meanwhile in the toilet, Sidebottom was still having a wee. He was facing backwards to the direction the plane was travelling in.

"Aaargh, noooo," he shouted as he fell backwards as the plane dived. His own wee sprayed back on top of him!

"Aargggh, I'm covered in my own wee!" he yelled, "yuearghh! There's wee everywhere!"

After a few more seconds the plane

levelled off.

"That idiot pilot, McPlop!" shouted Sidebottom.

Completely soaked, Sidebottom got to his feet and tried to dry himself with a towel.

He staggered out of the toilet in just his string vest and pants.

"Urggh," said a nearby passenger as she caught a whiff of Sidebottom.

"Aaaa!" Screamed an old lady who wasn't expecting to see a grown man walking down the plane in his pants.

In the cabin McPlop was laughing hysterically.

"Good job he packed plenty of clean pants," McPlop commented to no one in particular.

Sidebottom had meanwhile returned to the empty row of seats that he had been sitting at. He put his gravy soaked clothes down and moved over to the seat by the window. Suddenly the plane hit some turbulence and things got a little bumpy. In the cabin, McPlop was battling with the controls trying to keep the plane level. Then a warning light flashed on the dashboard. It read, 'Weight overload'.

"Ellen," said McPlop to the stewardess who had just joined him in the cabin, "this isn't good. We need to get rid of some weight from the plane otherwise we're going to crash."

"What do we get rid of?" said the stewardess, trying to sound calm, despite being very worried at the thought of crashing.

"We're going to have to throw out some of the luggage in the cargo hold. I want you to go down to the hold and move some luggage over to the cargo bay doors and then get yourself back up here to the cabin. I'll then open the cargo bay doors remotely from here and the luggage will get sucked out."

"Yes, Pilot McPlop."

"In the meantime I'll let the passengers know what's happening." McPlop picked up the radio to speak into. "This is your captain, the great pilot 'McPlop'," he announced. All the passengers quietened down and listened as he talked over the speaker. "There's some good news and some bad news. The good news is that we might be coming down to land sooner than expected. The bad news is: that this is going to happen because we're going to crash."

The passengers all started to panic and scream.

"But, I have a brilliant plan!" Continued the pilot. The passengers stopped panicking for a moment and all listened again. "If we get rid of some of the luggage in the cargo hold, then we might not crash because the plane won't be as heavy." The passengers all felt a little relieved that they weren't going to crash.

"Ha!" laughed Sidebottom to himself. "Some unlucky person's going to have his luggage thrown out of the plane." Sidebottom chuckled as he looked over at the people who had been laughing at him earlier when he had walked down the plane in his pants. "I hope it's one of them," he said, grinning slyly.

Whilst Pilot McPlop was making his life-saving announcement, Ellen the stewardess had made her way down to the cargo hold and after a few minutes the radio in the cabin crackled and her voice came over.

"Pilot McPlop, this is Ellen speaking. There's a lot of luggage down here, which luggage shall I move towards the cargo bay doors to be sucked out of the plane?"

McPlop's eyes suddenly lit up. He had just had a brilliant idea.

"Ellen, I want you to identify all the luggage that has the name 'Sidebottom' on it."

"I've found it all," said Ellen after a couple of minutes searching, "some awfully coloured luggage."

"Yes, that will be it. Okay move it over to the cargo bay doors and get yourself back up here."

A few minutes later Ellen had returned to the cabin. Pilot McPlop's hand was hovering over the, 'Open Cargo Door 2' button. He grinned at Ellen who had no idea why he was grinning at her.

"Jettison time!" he said with glee and hit the button. Cargo bay door 2, which was at the side of the plane near the wing, opened and all of Sidebottom's suitcases and luggage were sucked out of the plane, whacking the side of the door on their way out.

McPlop hit the 'Close Cargo Door 2' button.

Meanwhile a few of the passengers were watching the jettisoning of the luggage, from the safety of their windows.

"The luggage!" shouted one of the passengers who had watched it fly out of the cargo hold. "The suitcase must have hit the cargo door on the way out. It's split open and the clothes are flying all over the place!"

Sidebottom glanced out of the window so he could laugh at the contents of whoever's suitcase it was.

"Those suitcases look familiar," he pondered to himself. "Ha, look at all those pants flying everywhere."

Sidebottom frowned.

"Those brown pants look like a pair I've got. Hang on, so do those yellow and pink ones." Sidebottom stood up. "Hey, those are my pants!" He shouted. "And that's my luggage!" Sidebottom's face had turned red with fury. "McPlop!!!!" He yelled.

Meanwhile in the cabin, McPlop had heard Sidebottom shout his name.

"Urm…Ellen," said Pilot McPlop, "Please can you close the cabin door behind you and lock it very quickly." The pilot gave her a nervous smile.

"Yes, Pilot McPlop."

"And do you have that tazer gun near you? The one where you prod someone with it and it gives them an electric shock and sends them to sleep for half an hour."

"Yes, it's right by my chair."

"Good. If you see a madman dressed in a string vest and pants, who is trying to smash the cabin door down, then can you zap him."

"Of course, Pilot McPlop."

About ten seconds after Ellen has locked the cabin door behind her, a mad man dressed in a string vest and pants started hammering on the cabin door, shouting for the pilot.

"Open up, McPlop!" Shouted Sidebottom. "I want a word with you about my pants!"

Ellen saw Sidebottom and picked up her tazer and switched it on.

"BBZZZzzzzzz." Ellen pressed the button on the tazer as she prodded Sidebottom.

Sidebottom slumped down into a nearby chair and promptly fell asleep.

The stewardess knocked on the cabin door and McPlop let her in.

"That should keep him silent until we land, Pilot McPlop."

"Good work, Ellen. We'll be coming into land shortly."

About thirty minutes had passed and the plane had touched down at the airport and all the passengers had disembarked.

McPlop had decided to make a swift exit because Sidebottom was due to wake up at any moment.

"I'll see you later, Ellen," he said as he scurried out of the door.

"McPlop!" Came a shout from behind the pilot. McPlop turned around to see Sidebottom standing in his string vest. He had woken up and wasn't happy. "You owe me forty pairs of pants!" he shouted and started running after McPlop.

The last anyone saw of the pair was Sidebottom chasing McPlop down the runway and out of the airport shouting, "Pants, McPlop! I want my pants!"

## THE END

# Books by Adrian Lobley

### Kane series
Fictional books that also teach children about football history.

### The Football Maths Book series
Books that use fun football puzzles to help children with their maths (age range 4-9 years)

### A Learn to Read Book series
Books that use football and tennis to help children read their first words (ages 4-5 years)

For more information visit: www.adrianlobley.com

30320176R00072

Printed in Great
Britain
by Amazon